Hello, Family Members,

Learning to read is one of the most impo̶rtant accomplishments of early childhood. **Hello Reader!** books are designed to help children become skilled readers who like to read. Beginning readers learn to read by remembering frequently used words like "the," "is," and "and"; by using phonics skills to decode new words; and by interpreting picture and text clues. These books provide both the stories children enjoy and the structure they need to read fluently and independently. Here are suggestions for helping your child *before*, *during*, and *after* reading:

Before
- Look at the cover and pictures and have your child predict what the story is about.
- Read the story to your child.
- Encourage your child to chime in with familiar words and phrases.
- Echo read with your child by reading a line first and having your child read it after you do.

During
- Have your child think about a word he or she does not recognize right away. Provide hints such as "Let's see if we know the sounds" and "Have we read other words like this one?"
- Encourage your child to use phonics skills to sound out new words.
- Provide the word for your child when more assistance is needed so that he or she does not struggle and the experience of reading with you is a positive one.
- Encourage your child to have fun by reading with a lot of expression . . . like an actor!

After
- Have your child keep lists of interesting and favorite words.
- Encourage your child to read the books over and over again. Have him or her read to brothers, sisters, grandparents, and even teddy bears. Repeated readings develop confidence in young readers.
- Talk about the stories. Ask and answer questions. Share ideas about the funniest and most interesting characters and events in the stories.

I do hope that you and your child enjoy this book.

—Francie Alexander
Chief Education Officer,
Scholastic's Learning Ventures

For Rosie, a good egg
— M.D.R.

Go to scholastic.com for web site information on
Scholastic authors and illustrators.

ISBN 0-439-31418-6

Library of Congress Cataloging-in-Publication Data

Ramsey, Marcy Dunn.
    Eggs All Over / by Marcy Dunn Ramsey.
        p. cm.— (Hello reader! Level 1)
    "Cartwheel Books."
    Summary: Rhyming text and illustrations present many different eggs, including
brown and speckled blue eggs, snake and turtle eggs, penguin and spider eggs, and even
Humpty Dumpty.
    ISBN 0-439-31418-6 (pbk.)
    [1. Eggs—Fiction. 2. Stories in rhyme.] I. Title. II. Series.
PZ8.3.R146 Eg 2002
[E] — dc21   2001020185

10 9 8 7 6 5 4 3 2 1   02 03 04 05 06
                    Printed in the U.S.A.   24
                    First printing, May 2002

EGGS
ALL
OVER

by Marcy Dunn Ramsey

Hello Reader! — Level 1

SCHOLASTIC INC.

New York   Toronto   London   Auckland   Sydney
Mexico City   New Delhi   Hong Kong   Buenos Aires

There are white eggs,

brown eggs,

speckled eggs,

blue . . .

snake eggs,
turtle eggs,

gator eggs, too.

There are eggs underwater,

eggs up in trees,

eggs in the jungle,

and eggs that must not freeze!

There are eggs in the desert,

eggs from geese in France,

big eggs,

tiny eggs,

eggs that come from ants!

There are eggs brought by bunnies

and eggs bought in stores.

The biggest eggs that ever were came from dinosaurs!

Some eggs are under chickens

or on a bed of lace,

sitting up upon a wall,

or carried in a race.

No matter where you find them,

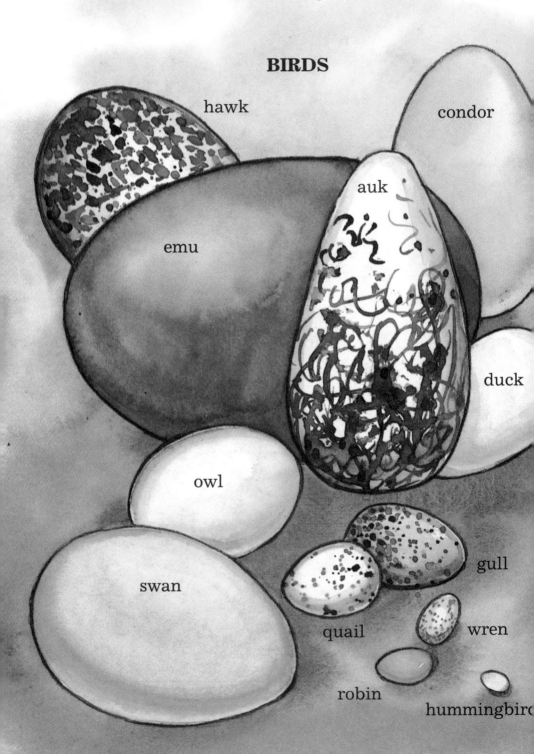

BIRDS

hawk

condor

auk

emu

duck

owl

swan

gull

quail

wren

robin

hummingbird

eggs are really neat.

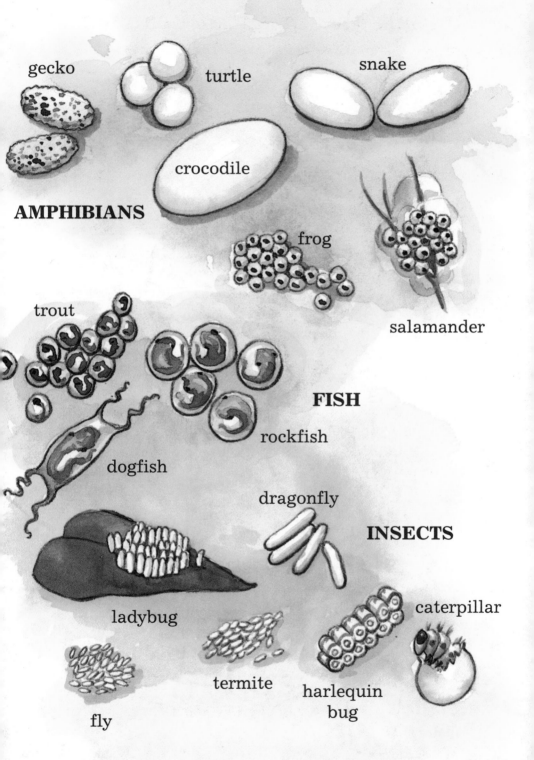

gecko

turtle

snake

crocodile

AMPHIBIANS

frog

salamander

trout

FISH

rockfish

dogfish

dragonfly

INSECTS

ladybug

caterpillar

termite

harlequin
bug

fly

But the best eggs of all
are the ones that I can eat!